The Wise Wind

by Fred Gerson
illustrated by Jeffrey Thompson

Harcourt
SCHOOL PUBLISHERS

Printed in China

ISBN 10: 0-15-350975-9
ISBN 13: 978-0-15-350975-9

Ordering Options
ISBN 10: 0-15-350601-6 (Grade 4 On-Level Collection)
ISBN 13: 978-0-15-350601-7 (Grade 4 On-Level Collection)
ISBN 10: 0-15-357928-5 (package of 5)
ISBN 13: 978-0-15-357928-8 (package of 5)

4 5 6 7 8 9 10 0940 12 11 10 09

As soon as he woke up, Brian Carver knew that it was another scorching day. Things were not going well at the Carver farm these days. The drought had stretched for weeks, putting the crops in danger of not growing large enough to sell.

Worse, Brian's father, Ted, was ill and wasn't able to do many of the chores. At fourteen, Brian would have preferred to spend time with his friends and do what other boys his age did. There was a lot to do to keep a farm going, though, and Brian only got away from his home occasionally.

Brian slowly got out of bed and treaded wearily downstairs. His father, like most days recently, was still in bed. His doctors weren't sure what was making him ill. His father couldn't stand being stuck in bed when there was so much to do around the farm. He felt like a hermit, barely leaving the house anymore.

"Good morning, Dad," Brian said cheerfully, entering his father's bedroom.

"Hi, son. Your mother's got some breakfast for you. Remember, today you need to mend the fences."

"I remember, Dad, and I'll take care of it," Brian said. He really wanted to make things better for his family.

After breakfast, Brian was feeling drab, but he tried not to think about his family's worries as he hiked along the fence. The sun was hot, but fortunately a slight breeze began to blow.

As Brian knelt down to take a closer look at a broken section of fence, he felt a stronger gust of wind hit him. Then, very faintly, he heard what he thought was a human voice, but he was the only person in the middle of a huge field. The wind blew, and again he heard what sounded like a soft voice, this time calling out his name—*Brian*.

"Well, that's mighty peculiar," Brian said to himself. He decided he must have been imagining things and got back to work.

Brian had repaired all of the wooden fence posts by midday and walked back to the house. His father greeted him at the door and said, "You're doing a nice job, son, and I really appreciate your help. I hope, soon enough, to be back out there myself."

"No problem, Dad. You're going to be well before you know it," Brian replied.

His mother had made a nice lunch. "Brian..." she called out from the kitchen. As soon as he heard his name, he remembered the voice in the wind—*Brian*.

The next day, Brian's father asked him to inspect the crops. Brian headed out to the middle of the field in the hot sun. When he was looking at the frail cornstalks, a gust of wind came up, and with it came that same, soft voice—*Brian*. Brian looked up and around and saw no one. Thinking he must not have been imagining things, he decided to answer back.

"What?" Brian said.

Hello, said the wind.

Brian stopped in his tracks, trembling with fear. "This is too weird," he said to himself. "It can't be happening." Then he decided that there was an easy way to find out more about this situation: he could just answer back again.

"Uh, hello," Brian said timidly.

Hello, Brian, said the wind.

Now Brian knew he wasn't hearing things—he knew he was really hearing the wind speak to him, and it even knew his name. "Or does it?" Brian thought. "Maybe it just sounds like my name. Maybe it's just a wind blowing through the corn, and it makes an odd sound." He decided to test his idea.

"You know, I'm Ray, not Brian," he said to the wind.

Very funny, Brian, the wind said. Brian looked around again and then started to laugh. The wind was actually speaking to him.

When he returned to the house that day to have dinner, Brian thought about telling his parents about his odd experience but decided against it. Besides, he had enough bad news to tell them: the plants were doing very badly, and if it didn't rain soon, the entire crop could be lost.

Brian wished more than anything that he could somehow make the situation better for his family. Then a moment later, a strange idea popped into his head: he would ask the wind for help.

The next morning, Brian went back out to the field. He didn't want anyone near him when he tried to speak with the wind. He looked around and said, "Wind?"

Suddenly, a brief gust of wind blew, and Brian heard the words, *Yes, Brian?*

"My father is ill and isn't getting better, so what should I do?" he asked.

Still means ill, said the wind. Brian didn't know what that meant and was about to ask the wind to explain. Then the breeze stopped blowing, and Brian realized that the wind had gone.

Though the message from the wind was strange, Brian was thrilled that at least he had something to think about. He dashed home, deep in thought, and he found his father sitting on the front porch. *Still means ill* went through Brian's mind again, but what could it mean?

"I'll be right back, Dad. I have to put something in the house," Brian said. While inside, Brian thought more about *still means ill*. Suddenly, something dawned on him: maybe it wasn't good for his father to be still all the time. The wind was saying that Brian's father would get better sooner if he went out more.

"Dad, I'd like you to come and examine the work I did on the fence posts," Brian said, coming out of the house. His father looked at him, surprised, and then smiled and got up. Brian and his father slowly walked out to inspect the fences. Brian made sure to go at an easy pace so that his father wouldn't get too exhausted. Brian was surprised to see that, as they walked, his father seemed more energetic.

"You know, I'm feeling better, kid," his father said with a smile.

For the next week, Brian and his father took walks together around the farm, and his father slowly began to regain his strength. Brian was fascinated by his father's progress. Within two weeks, his father's health improved dramatically, and he was able to accomplish more and more around the farm. Everything was looking better for Brian, the family, and the farm. The only thing that was still a problem was the drought. They still needed a few good rains to keep the plants strong. Brian knew what he had to do.

"Wind?" Brian said, standing alone in the field one afternoon. The sun was hot, and there had still been no rain. Suddenly, Brian felt a breeze.

Yes, Brian? said the wind.

"We need some rain to save the crops," Brian said, feeling funny that he was asking the wind for a favor.

Umbrella, said the wind, and Brian smiled— he didn't have to think too hard to figure out what that meant.

"Thank you," said Brian, walking toward the house. Within minutes, the sky darkened and rain began to fall.

Life for Brian's family improved from that day on. He never knew why the wind had helped him, but every time he felt a cool breeze, he was thankful that it had.

Think Critically

1. What do you think would have happened if the rain had not come?

2. How would you describe Brian?

3. How could Brian tell that the wind was really speaking to him?

4. What does *still means ill* mean?

5. Do you think that the wind was really speaking to Brian? Explain your answer.

 Language Arts

Finish the Story Write some more of the story, telling what happened when the rain finally came and how it helped Brian and his family.

School-Home Connection Share this story with a family member. Then talk about what you would do if you had to take on the responsibilities that Brian had.

Word Count: 1,228